The Game

Philip M. Fishman

The Game

© by Philip M. Fishman 2022
Published by MPS Publishing
ISBN 978-0-9891708-7-1

All rights reserved. No part of this book other than cover images for review purposes only may be reproduced or transmitted in any form or by any means, electronic or mechanical, including photocopying, recording, or any other information storage and retrieval system, without the written permission of the author, who may be reached at fishmanpm@gmail.com.

Design of front and back cover are by Dee Marley of White Rabbit Arts Historical Fiction Company

Foreword

In *The Game*, Philip Fishman masterfully creates a story with amazing coincidences that are surprisingly believable. He presents us with characters who are truth-seekers, unafraid of what they might find out, as they shine a light on the terror and violence perpetrated by a former SS officer who has settled nicely into Albany, New York, ironically masquerading as a Jewish immigrant from the Holocaust that he was a part of. The character development is superb. You will love Alex and Rivka and you will detest Stahl. As you read, you will be crying at times, and laughing or cheering at times, and at least at one point, you will probably be doing two of the three at the same time.

By deftly weaving historical accuracies of Nazi Germany (and particularly the events of Kristallnacht) with fiction, the book offers a tableau of the family secrets of three young adults and, in particular, one man's journey to right—or at least provide an appropriate and satisfying response to—tragic wrongs that were typical of the atrocities of the time.

If our shared human history is any indication, hatred and "otherness" will never be eradicated. But stories like these (not "stories," though, in a *literary* sense; these are the accountings of true events and the potential for one such thread to come to the conclusion it deserves) serve to remind us that this horrific chapter cannot be erased, nor should it be. We share the responsibility of constant vigilance to ensure that such unspeakable acts and the blind hate and prejudice they originated from are fought wherever they occur.

Fortunately, I had no close family members who experienced the horrors of the Holocaust, but as Fishman points out, every Jew has a family connection to that terrible time.

Never forget.

- Debbie Burke, author of *Klezmer for the Joyful Soul*

The Game

Table of Contents

Prologue 11
Chapter One 13
Chapter Two 17
Chapter Three 20
Chapter Four 21
Chapter Five 23
Chapter Six 25
Chapter Seven 33
Chapter Eight 36
Chapter Nine 46
Chapter Ten 48
Chapter Eleven 52
Chapter Twelve 55
Chapter Thirteen 63
Chapter Fifteen 78
Chapter Sixteen 82
Epilogue 83
Acknowledgments 86

The Game

"Mind your own business." An adage with deep philosophical roots in British and American libertarianism. A version of it was actually the motto on the reverse side of the first coin minted by the United States in 1787, the Fugio Cent.

There are even Biblical references: In 1 Thessalonians 4:11-12, Paul states that believers should "...lead a quiet life...mind your own business." And in Romans 13-1, "Let every person be subject to the governing authorities. For there is no authority except from God, and those that exist have been instituted by God."

But there are times when one must stand up and say "NO!" When a government or authority is illegitimate as evidenced by its sanctioning and committing murder, thievery, propaganda, disenfranchising a segment of the population, and turning one segment against another, one must no longer mind his own business. Rather, his business is then everyone's business, and becomes one of resistance.

"First they came for the socialists, and I did not speak out — because I was not a socialist.

"Then they came for the trade unionists, and I did not speak out — because I was not a trade unionist.

"Then they came for the Jews, and I did not speak out — because I was not a Jew.

"Then they came for me — and there was no one left to speak for me." Pastor Martin Niemoller

Prologue

I was almost six years old when I began seeing newsreels at the movies of the liberation of the death camps and horrific carnage at the conclusion of the war. I was, of course, far too young to fully grasp what it was all about, but I didn't require an adult mind to know that it was terrible.

I recall asking Mom what a concentration camp was. I knew that to concentrate meant to think hard. She began crying as she replied, "Honey, they were terrible places. Places where your Bubba and Zada's mommy and daddy were killed."

"Little Bubba and Little Zada?" (Bubba and Zada are Yiddish for grandmother and grandfather, respectively. The little meant they were my maternal grandparents. They also just happened to be shorter than my paternal grandparents.)

"Yes, but Big Bubba and Big Zada's mommy and daddy and uncles and aunts too." I learned much later that my Aunt Toba Kudek, who was Little Bubba's younger sister, had been rescued from a camp at the conclusion of the war.

Six million of my fellow Jews were murdered in those camps between 1941 and 1945, my ancestors, uncles, aunts, and cousins. Every Jew alive today had countless relatives put to death for one reason only, their religion. Even if they had never been to a synagogue or temple or practiced one of the ancient traditions. If he or she had three grandparents whose genealogy was one hundred percent Jewish, that person was considered Jewish. We were a race to be extinguished by Hitler and his madmen. Those who had only one or two Jewish grandparents were referred to as Mischlinge (mixed race), who were discriminated against and treated poorly, but not nearly to the degree of Jews.

This was the Holocaust that some deny ever happened. But we must never forget. When I hear one of those deniers state that it

The Game

was all a lie, just Jewish propaganda, does it make me angry? You're damn right it does. I wish it were possible to take those idiots back in time to personally witness the carnage and stench. I would have them pick up each of those corpses by hand and give each a proper burial.

After the camps were liberated with photographs showing the grisly conditions, most of the townspeople surrounding the camps said they had no idea that such atrocities had taken place right in their figurative backyard. Ike (President Eisenhower) and Allied commanders correctly had many of them tour the camps to see for themselves to sear it into their memories so that they would never forget.

This is a work of fiction with a flashback to that horrific period of time. Most of the current-day narrative is imagination, but too much of the flashback is based on the truth. We must never forget.

Chapter One

It must have been a quirk of fate. That's the only way to explain it.

It was August 2, 1960 on Alex Greenbaum's 21st birthday when he drove his brand-new red Studebaker convertible to Albany to join a stockbroker agency that was managed by a fraternity friend of his father. That he had made that choice was inexplicable to his parents because he had a fabulous offer from a prestigious finance company in Manhattan, but they did not argue with his decision. The car was a combination birthday present and reward for finishing magna cum laude with a degree in finance from Yale.

Since he was new to the city, his boss invited him to dinner at his home to meet his wife and daughter, and Alex graciously accepted. Nate Levinson had warned his family to stay away from the subject of Alex's adoption as it might be a sensitive subject.

It was early in the evening with still a lot of daylight when Alex pulled up to the Levinson house. Nate came out to greet his new employee and introduce him to his family. He remarked on the nice "set of wheels."

"Thanks. A birthday gift from my folks."

Nate's wife, Rivka, had followed her husband outside and asked, "So, today's your birthday?"

"Yes, 21 today."

Rivka's eyes widened, but she replied, "Nate should have told me so that I could've baked a cake."

Alex chuckled, "No problem. It's enough of a birthday present to have dinner with you and your family."

Over dinner, Alex was intrigued to find so much in common with his new employer's family, and Rivka seemed similarly intrigued in the conversation. She would have liked to ask if Alex knew the town where he had been adopted but deferred upon her husband's advice.

Levinson and Alex's adoptive father had formed a close friendship during their days at Yale, having been roommates with both majoring in finance.

Alex knew about the Yale connection and friendship, but what he did not know is that both men had been in the Army and stationed in England during WWII. Levinson and Alex's father had both met and married their wives there. Levinson and his wife left at the conclusion of the war, but Greenbaum and his wife remained there for almost another year.

Steve Greenbaum had been severely wounded during the Allied invasion on D-Day and evacuated to England several days later. His right leg up to the hip had to be amputated, and he was fitted with a prosthesis. Then began months of grueling therapy. Nancy Wakefield, a young nurse who had just finished her therapy certification, was assigned to work with him until his release from the hospital on Christmas Day 1945. That afternoon the rehab nurse and patient were married, although both were aware that because of Steve's injury, they would be unable to have natural children. And so began the search for an adoptive child.

After visiting a number of orphanages in and around London, they met and fell in love with the six-year-old Alex. All they knew at the time was that he had been born out of wedlock and that his young mother had placed him in the orphanage as an infant. It was only a few months later, after a lot of record searching, that they found out that Alex's mother had been Jewish, but that presented no problem since Steve was also of Jewish ancestry. Alex therefore was at least 50% Jewish, the same as what the offspring of Steve and Nancy would have been if they had been able to have children.

Levinson's wife, Rivka, was born in Germany, but became a naturalized British citizen after being sent to England on the Kindertransport after Kristallnacht. Being fluent in German as well as English, she was recruited as a cryptographer and worked at

Bletchley Park where she met Nate, who worked in Army Intelligence. Since marriage, she held dual citizenship with the U.S., the same as Alex.

Rivka and Nate had married in June 1942, and their daughter, Marsha, was born in March 1943. Alex was certainly interested in the conversation with his new boss and family, but he had a hard time keeping his eyes off the beautiful, dark-haired Marsha. The attraction appeared to be mutual to the dark and handsome Alex but didn't go unnoticed by her parents. They too were impressed with Alex but were feeling that Marsha was too young for a romantic relationship, particularly with someone four years older.

Marsha had picked up a vocabulary of a hundred or so German words from her mother over the years of growing up, but since her father didn't speak it, there was little spoken, and it was not until she was in high school that she became interested in learning her mother's native language. Her first day in high school, she met Ingrid Goldberg, who was to become her best friend. She had been born in Germany, was an only child like Marsha, and in addition to their German background, their families were both secular Jews.

Furthermore, the two girls bore an amazing resemblance that some mistook for a sibling relationship.

Herr Goldberg had emigrated from Germany with his wife and daughter after the war and had been teaching German at Theodore Roosevelt High School in Albany since 1950. Goldberg was a strict disciplinarian and was quick to drop students who were not serious about learning the language.

However, he was the only German teacher, and there were plenty of kids interested in learning the language of their heritage.

Early Albany had a strong Germanic influence, but with the discrimination against anything German due to the two world wars, assimilation, and intermarriage, spoken German in the area had almost vanished. Still, there were vestiges of the culture in food and beer, and by the 1950s, things began coming back.

The Game

Goldberg was a very private person, and students didn't know much about him other than the rumors of his having been in a concentration camp. One thing they knew for sure was that he had an extreme distaste for being photographed. Two years earlier, a student tried to get a picture of herself and Goldberg. She had just received the camera for her birthday and lent it to a friend to snap the picture. Goldberg grabbed the camera from the friend's hands, threw it on the floor, and smashed it with his foot. She and her friend cried, but all he had to say was, "No photographs." How he had managed to survive or where his wife and son had been during the war, no one knew.

Chapter Two

Heinrich Stahl had been a student at Humboldt University in Professor Schoenstein's Advanced English class in 1935, shortly before the enactment of the Nuremberg Laws. Schoenstein was an excellent but demanding teacher, and therefore admired by most of his students, but not by Stahl.

The incident occurred early in the spring semester when Stahl had been called upon to comment on one of Shakespeare's passages. Stahl was one of those high-IQ students who did little homework in any of his classes and preferred to "wing" it, generally resulting in the humiliation of many of his teachers. But Stahl had grossly underestimated Schoenstein's intelligence, and the tables were turned as Stahl made a fool of himself with the entire class laughing at him.

Schoenstein had asked Stahl if he could comment on Shakespeare's character, Touchstone, in the play Macbeth. Stahl responded after a slight pause, "Touchstone was a pretty minor character, who, in my opinion, contributed little to the plot."

The professor responded, "Congratulations, Stahl.

Touchstone was indeed a very minor character in Macbeth. In fact, he was so minor that he didn't even appear in that play. What Touchstone is famous for is his quote in the play, As You Like It. 'The fool doth think he is wise, but the wise man knows himself to be a fool.'"

From that day on, Stahl vowed to avenge his humiliation.

In September, when Schoenstein, along with other Jewish members of the faculty, were discharged, Stahl had a big laugh, but he still was not satisfied. Stahl had been a member of Hitler Youth since its early days, long before Hitler came to power, and therefore had risen in rank to one of von Schirach's key lieutenants. Upon graduation, on the basis of his military training, Stahl was

The Game

commissioned a Captain in the SS. By 1938, Stahl had achieved the rank of Lieutenant Colonel and on November 9 of that year, he finally got his revenge.

Schoenstein, his wife, and teenage daughter were no longer in the privileged upper middle class of society. Since his dismissal from the university, the family had subsisted on savings and the meager earnings from teaching English to other Jews who could afford to pay anything. In fact, several of his students were gratis. Previously, the family had lived in a fine house in one of Berlin's exclusive neighborhoods. Now, they were living in a two-room apartment with the lavatory, tub, and toilet separated from the bedroom by a shower curtain. The second small bed was in the other room, which served as a combination living room/bedroom/kitchen.

It was 7:00 in the evening with the Schoensteins having dinner when a hard knock was heard. "Offen, Juden." Schoenstein complied by opening the door to see an SS officer accompanied by two enlisted men.

"Do you remember me, Herr Professor?"

"Yes, I do. Stahl."

"Correction, Jude. It is Oberstleutnant Stahl."

"Ah, I see, Lieutenant Colonel Stahl. My former student has done quite well for himself."

"Yes, he has, and I might add, with no help from you. On the other hand, look at you."

"Yes, thanks to your bastard leader, Hitler, who will rot in hell with the rest of you scum."

Infuriated, Stahl slapped the professor's face. "Herr Professor, you will live to regret that remark, and then, maybe not." He then turned to his men. "Go through the apartment, including the drawers. Bring me anything that appears valuable." He then turned back to Schoenstein. "Herr Professor, we are now going to play a little game. You will have the choice as to whom I will have sex with tonight, your wife or your daughter."

"You swine. I refuse to participate in your hellish game."

"Nein, Herr Professor, you will participate. The second rule of the game is that if you do not exercise your choice, I will first kill your wife, and then have sex with your daughter."

"You are a madman."

"So that is your choice, Schoenstein?" Stahl said as he pointed the Luger at Mrs. Schoenstein's head.

The daughter spoke up. "Herr Oberstleutnant, come with me into the bedroom."

"Schoenstein, you have a very intelligent and beautiful daughter," he said as he and the girl headed into the bedroom. "Schoenstein, you and your wife may continue your meal." And then to his men, "Stand guard while I attend to some business in the next room."

Chapter Three

It was five years later in early summer that Stahl, now Oberst Stahl since his latest promotion, and Schoenstein were to meet again. This time it was at the Dachau Concentration Camp. Both the professor and his wife had been arrested months earlier for the writing and distribution of anti-Nazi leaflets. The two were separated upon entry to the camp and Mrs. Schoenstein sent to the gas chamber. Schoenstein and several other men were spared immediate extermination to work in a nearby munitions factory.

Stahl had just been assigned to the camp as Commandant when he spotted the name of his old nemesis, Moshe Schoenstein. "So the esteemed professor has elected to help the war effort?"

"Go to hell, Stahl."

"Some respect for Kommandant Stahl," he said as he slapped Schoenstein's face. "You and your co-workers will remain alive as long as it suits me. Any more disrespect from you, and I will be executing one of you at a time."

Schoenstein spit in Stahl's face.

"So you disbelieve me," he said as he put his Luger up against the head of the man closest to him. "What is your name, Jew?"

"Haim Goldberg."

"Verabschiede dich, Goldberg," he said as he pulled the trigger.

Chapter Four

Rivka Levinson had a hard time sleeping that night. There was something about Alex that she could not get out of her mind. The next morning, as soon as Nate left for the office, she dialed information.

"Yes, may I help you?"

"Yes. Boston, Mass, for the Steve Greenbaum residence." When she got the number, she pondered. What was she going to say? After a minute or two, she dialed.

"Hello."

"Hi. You must be Nancy."

"Yes, and who is this?"

"Nancy, my name is Rivka Levinson. We've never met, but our husbands are good friends dating back to their time at Yale."

"Of course. Your husband is Nate, and you live in Albany, NY."

"Exactly. I had the pleasure of meeting your son, Alex, last night over dinner and just wanted to tell you how impressed we were with him. I'm sure that he will be a great asset to Nate's business."

"Thank you. Yes, he is a remarkable young man, although I have to confess that we were disappointed that he didn't take the position with the investment firm in Manhattan."

"I totally understand, but you should be happy that you have a son who thinks for himself."

"Absolutely. We raised him that way, and now we have to accept the consequences." Nancy chuckled.

Rivka chuckled back, but in the meantime, she was thinking, *This is a very nice conversation that we're having, but how in the heck do I get around to asking her what I need to know?* As she pondered, Nancy gave her the opening that she was looking for.

The Game

"As you probably know, Alex was adopted, but we couldn't love him more if he were our natural child."

"Naturally, and you and your husband should be very proud of the man he has become."

"We are."

"I assume that you must have visited several orphanages before you found your Alex?"

"Oh yes. Probably dozens,"

"Had you already decided before you met him that you wanted a boy of a particular age?"

"We did want a boy to continue Steve's family name. No age in particular, but we didn't want an infant. Not too young and not too old, kind of like a male Goldilocks." Nancy chuckled, and Rivka joined in.

She hesitated but finally dove in. "Where did you say that you found him?"

"I don't think I did, but it was an orphanage in a village just north of Oxford where I grew up. I can't recall its name..."

Damn. Rivka bit her lip but was happy that Nancy was unable to see her reaction.

"Oh yes. It just came to me. It was in the village of Middleton Chesney."

In the midst of conflicting emotions, Rivka responded, "Yes, it's funny how things will come back to us after we've thought we had forgotten them. But Nancy, it's been a delight to talk to you. I hope that we will be able to get together at some future point."

After they had hung up, Rivka pondered over the conversation. She really liked Nancy, and she was relieved that she had been able to get the information she was looking for, but at the same time disappointed that the answer wasn't the one she had hoped it would be.

Chapter Five

The Levinsons were having dinner when the phone rang. Marsha ran to pick it up. She had been hoping that Alex would call, but it had been three days, and she had almost given up.

"Hello."

"Hi, this is Alex from a few nights ago. I assume that this is Marsha?"

"You got it... I mean her."

"Great. You probably know about the rock concert at the amphitheater tomorrow night?"

"Sure. My good friend Ingrid and I are planning on going."

"I see. I was hoping to take you."

"No problem. You can take both of us."

"Sounds good. Shall I come by at 6:30?"

"We'll be here and waiting." Marsha came back to the dinner table with a big smile.

Rivka spoke. "Must have been a good phone call?"

"Yes, it was Alex. He wanted to take me to the concert, but it will be a double date, sort of."

Nate was just sitting back listening while Rivka continued the conversation. "Can you translate?"

"It's not complicated. Ingrid and I were planning on going to the rock concert tomorrow evening, and now it'll be a threesome instead of just us two."

Nate spoke up now. "Sweetie, your mother and I really like Alex, but don't you think he's a bit old for you?"

"Come on, Dad. As I recall, Mom was only nineteen when you married her, and how old were you at the time?"

Rivka responded," You're comparing apples and oranges. It was war time, and besides, I was almost twenty."

The Game

"Well, don't worry. We're only going out to a concert, not getting married, and Ingrid will be kind of like a chaperone."

Nate responded, "And, who will chaperone Ingrid?"

Marsha chuckled.

After dinner, she placed a call to Ingrid, who answered. "Hi, Ingrid. Can you drive over tomorrow evening?"

"I thought you were driving this time?"

"I know, but something has come up. I'll explain tomorrow."

"We're still on for the concert, aren't we?" "For sure, but there is a slight complication."

"Weird."

"Don't worry. You will totally understand. Gotta run right now. See you at around 6:25."

Chapter Six

Ingrid drove up right on time and honked. Marsha came out and told her to park, get out of the car, and await their ride.

"What ride?"

"You'll see."

About that time Alex drove up. "Hi Marsha. Who's your beautiful friend?"

Marsha forced a smile. "Alex, my beautiful friend is Ingrid, and she will be going with us to the concert."

"That's great. I'll bet I will be the only fellow there with two beautiful dates."

Ingrid quickly responded, "I'll bet Marsha and I will be the only two beautiful women sharing one handsome fella."

"Marsha, your friend is not only beautiful, but witty." He opened the front door and the two girls slid into the front seat. Marsha was happy to be in the middle and was trying to think of something to say but was beginning to think that introducing Alex to Ingrid may not have been a great idea.

"So tell me Alex, how do you happen to know Marsha?"

"I just came down to work for her father."

"From Boston, I take it?"

"Yeah, I guess my accent gave that away."

Marsha tried unsuccessfully to break into the conversation. "Our families go way back."

"So what's the connection between Albany and Boston?"

"College and the war."

"Can you explain?"

Marsha was beginning to feel ill. "Alex, can you pull over at the next gas station?"

Alex obliged, Ingrid got out, and Marsha dashed to the restroom. "Must have been something she ate. So tell me about the 'college and war' connection."

The Game

Alex explained, and by the time Marsha had gotten back to the car, Ingrid was sitting next to him, and it appeared that the two were old friends.

Ingrid greeted her friend, "You're back. We missed you."

"I'll bet."

The ride to and from the concert was unusually quiet. Alex dropped the two girls at Marsha's house, and said, "Thank you both for allowing me to come with you. I really enjoyed it. "

Ingrid responded, "Thanks, Alex. It was our pleasure."

After he drove off, Ingrid attempted to thank her friend for the introduction but was rebuffed as Marsha rushed into her home crying. Ingrid took the cue and left in her car.

Marsha's parents were waiting up for her watching the late news. Rivka saw her first. "Darling, whatever is the matter?"

"I would rather not talk about it. May I just go to bed?"

"Have you eaten?"

"No, but I'm not hungry."

Her mother followed her up the steps to her room. "Please tell me."

"It's Ingrid, Mom." As soon as she got the words out, there was a gush of tears.

"Did something happen to her?"

"No, Mom. Apparently, she's been like that all along. I just didn't know."

"Like what, honey?"

"Mom, may I just go to bed?"

"Certainly, honey." She kissed her daughter goodnight.

She left her daughter's room, headed down the steps, and heard her husband. "What in hell was that all about?"

"I'm not sure, Nate. Something about Ingrid."

"Was she hurt?"

"No. Some kind of quarrel between the two."

"Okay. Typical teenage stuff."

Rivka's female intuition told her that Alex was involved in Marsha's upset, but said nothing more about it.

That night, Rivka had a dream where she ran into her grown son at a train station. They boarded the train and sat down next to each other. She asked him where he was going, and he replied that he was going to find his mother. She asked him where she lived, and he replied that he didn't know. She also didn't know where she was going.

When she awoke the next morning, she tried to recall much more about her dream but was unable. She made the decision to tell her husband about the strange dream and to share a secret with him that she had kept to herself all these years of marriage.

They were at their customarily early breakfast, and Rivka knew that Marsha wouldn't be down for at least a couple of hours since she always slept late on Saturdays. And with the upset of the night before, she might be even later in coming down.

"Nate, I would like to tell you about a weird dream I had last night."

"OK, I hope it's entertaining."

"I don't know about that, but I think it might be tied into something I've been thinking." She then related to him as much as she could remember about the dream.

"You're right. It was crazy, but no more so than most. But you said also that it could be related to something on your mind."

"Yes, darling. Please don't get mad at me."

"Jeez, Rivka. Are you going to tell me that you have a mad crush on a movie star?"

Rivka tensed up and felt the perspiration on her face, pausing before answering. "No, nothing like that... I was raped when I was sixteen..."

Nate's facial expression went from inquisitive to sad as he rose and hugged her tightly. "I'm so sorry, honey. I'm so sorry."

"Nate, I'm the one that's sorry. I know that I should have told you."

The Game

"Honey, it's OK. I understand."

Rivka relaxed slightly to have that part of the revelation out of the way, but wasn't sure how Nate would respond to the rest of it, "Thank you, but there is more... I became pregnant and had a son..."

Nate sat back down with his eyes widened. "So where is he?"

"That's the $64,000 question. I think that I don't know."

"You think that you don't know? What kind of answer is that?"

"I'm just not sure..."

The phone rang and gave Rivka a chance to break the tension. She ran to get it, and it was Ingrid.

"Hi, Mrs. Levinson, may I speak to Marsha?"

"She's still up in her room. Let me get her for you."

"If it's not too much trouble."

"No, she should come down for breakfast anyway." Rivka looked back at Nate with a sorrowful expression as she went up the stairs. She knocked on Marsha's door. "Sweetie, Ingrid's on the phone."

"Mom, can you tell her I'm sick?"

"No, Marsha. You know better than that. Come down and face the music."

"All right. Tell her I'll be down as soon as I get something on."

Rivka came back to the table, hoping that the time interval had broken the uncomfortable dialogue, but Nate interrupted the thought, "You were saying?"

"I just don't know..."

"But you think you might know?"

"It's crazy, Nate, but I have this gnawing sense that Alex may be my son."

"What?" Nate gave her an incredulous look after spilling his coffee.

"I know. It sounds absurd, but there are so many things..."

Nate extended his palms. "Like what?"

"Haven't you noticed how much Alex resembles Marsha?"

"So that's it?"

"No, Nate, that's not it. Alex is an orphan, born in England on the same day that my son was born."

"That still doesn't prove anything. There are coincidences everywhere, and to think that this fellow who just came into our lives is your son is beyond preposterous."

"I know."

Before Nate could respond, Marsha appeared after finishing her call with Ingrid.

Nate asked, "So what was that all about last night?"

"Nothing really."

Nate continued, "It sure seemed like something..."

Rivka interrupted, "Nate, let's let Marsha have some breakfast, and then if she cares to talk about it..."

"It's OK, Mom. It was just a misunderstanding between Ingrid and me. It's all cleared up now."

Nate started to say something, but Rivka signaled him to defer. No more was said about last night or about Rivka's suspicion. Nevertheless, Rivka could not put the thought out of her mind. There was one other thing she could check, but she wasn't sure how to go about it.

The opportunity presented itself less than two months later, as luck would have it. Rivka read the announcement in the Thursday paper as she and Nate were having breakfast. "Nate, Red Cross is having their annual blood drive this Saturday, and I think I would like to go since I do have a pretty rare blood type."

"That's fine. Since you don't like football that much, I'm planning on driving down to New Haven with Alex for Yale's first game of the season."

"What time's the game?"

"You want to go?"

"No, I just wondered when you would be leaving."

The Game

"The game's at 2:00 and I figured we could grab a late lunch around 1:00 or so. It's a two-and-a-half-hour drive, so we should leave around 10:30. Why the interest in our departure time?"

"I thought we could go to the blood drive together and since Alex..."

Nate paused before responding, and then it hit him. "You're just not going to let that thing go. I guess I will humor you, but will you finally realize that you are just chasing a wild dream when his blood type comes up with something other than AB negative?"

"Yes, thank you, darling." She kissed him on the cheek, feeling relieved.

"OK. We'll get down there early and hope that there isn't a long line, but here's the deal. Alex will be picking me up, so we'll go in two cars. If we can't be done by 10:00, you can go ahead and donate your blood. Alex and I will be off to New Haven."

"Fair enough."

The two cars arrived together Saturday a little bit after 8:30. Rivka was thankful that the line was not long. Rivka spoke. "So, big day for two Yalies?"

"Yes ma'am. Yale shouldn't have too much of a problem with UConn but one never knows."

"Yes, I suppose that's what makes the game interesting. Have you ever donated blood before?"

"Yes, ma'am. Many times. My blood type is said to be the rarest..."

It was one of those warm-up games in early season. No one had expected Connecticut to have a chance against a strong Yale team, and there were no surprises. But even if it had been an exciting match, Nate would have had a hard time in staying focused on the game. Instead, he was thinking about the implications of Alex's statement on his blood type.

Could that too be one of the many coincidences?

When Nate got home that evening after dropping Alex off and waiting till Marsha retired to her room, he and Rivka had a long discussion on the ramifications of the latest discovery and what they should do about it, if anything. "Rivka, darling, you have me finally believing that it might be so, but even if it is true, what do you figure we need to do about it?"

At last, feeling vindicated, she restrained herself from an 'I told you so' and responded, "I don't know, Nate, but it's just something that I need to know."

"Do you realize how silly that sounds? You don't know what you will do with the information, but you need to have it."

"I suppose to you it may sound insane, but Nate, he may be my son."

"All right, darling. I can see that you aren't going to put this away until you are absolutely convinced, one way or another. What do you propose?"

"I would like to go to England."

"I was afraid of that. With or without me?"

"I would love for us to go together, but if you can't break away from your brokerage for a few days, I will understand."

"I think Alex could handle things for a few days, but what about Marsha?"

"On second thought, maybe you should stay behind."

"So, what do we tell our daughter?"

"Let me think on that."

Later that night when they were in bed, Rivka jostled her husband awake. "Nate, I've got it!"

"Wha--?"

"Bletchley."

"You're not making sense. Are you still asleep?"

"No. That will be the reason that I'm going to England. Lillian Ratchford was my best friend at Bletchley. She found me here in Albany and asked me to come and visit."

"Do you think Marsha will buy that?"

The Game

"Why not? I'm going back to sleep now, and I'll come up with enough backstory to make it convincing. Sorry I woke you. Go back to sleep."

The next morning at breakfast, Rivka exclaimed, "I had the most thrilling call last night after the two of you were sound asleep. Lillian Ratchford, my best friend during my code-breaking days during the war, somehow found me in Albany and asked me to come visit her in England. She has been in touch with several of our mutual friends, and we are going to have a reunion to catch up on everyone's lives."

Nate responded first, "We are going to have a reunion? You're planning on going to England?"

"We all can go. You can take Marsha around and show her the sights while I catch up with the girls."

Marsha spoke, "How long would we be staying?"

"I don't know. Maybe two or three weeks."

"What about my brokerage?"

"Can't Alex handle it?"

"We've got a lot of clients that Alex hasn't even met yet. I just don't think this is such a good idea."

Marsha agreed, "Mom, why don't you go and enjoy yourself? Dad and I can manage for a while without you."

"Nate, what do you think?"

"If you must, then do it. I'm sure that you will have some lovely stories to relate when you get back."

"All right then. I will call a travel agent and start getting packed."

Chapter Seven

Three days later, Rivka arrived at London's Gatwick airport at 6:40 a.m. Although it had been one of those red-eye flights, eleven hours in total with a change in planes at LaGuardia, she was so excited that she had barely slept. She was certain now that Alex was her son, and her mission was to prove it. But she knew there would be roadblocks since orphanages were notorious for keeping their records confidential.

She would need help and decided that her first outreach would be to her old friend, Lillian Ratchford. The story about her friend contacting her had been untrue, but it was a fact that the two had been best friends as cryptographers at Bletchley.

All of the code-breakers had one thing in common: they were resourceful. Rivka had not been in contact with her friend in fifteen years, and therefore had no idea where she lived. Complicating things further was the probability that Lillian had married in the intervening years and was now going by her married name. What she did know was that Lillian was from Reading, so that is where she would start.

Rivka rented one of the small British cars and was off to the short drive to Reading. It had been a long time since she had been in a car with the steering wheel on the right side and having to drive on the left side of the road, but she had little difficulty in re-learning. She knew that turns could be problematic and that she would have to concentrate to stay on the right side, the correct side, of the road.

Stopping at a gas station when she entered Reading, she got directions to the library. She got a local phone book and looked up Ratchford.

No Lillians, but there were six Ratchfords, and she proceeded to call them. The first one, A.E., didn't answer. A woman at the

The Game

David Ratchford number answered, but she was of no help. The woman was David's widow, and they had been married thirty years when he died two years earlier. She knew a number of Ratchfords, all of whom lived outside Reading except for one. Most of them she had lost track of and had no idea where to find them.

After calling the rest of the numbers and finding no connection to Lillian, Rivka decided to check hospital birth records. She didn't know when Lillian was born, but recalled that her birthday was close to Christmas since they had joked about her missing out on gifts for that reason. She assumed that they were about the same age and after a couple of hours of searching, she found Lillian Ratchford, born on December 24, 1920. Her parents were Randolph and Beth. There were no Randolph Ratchfords in the Reading telephone directory, so he was either deceased or had moved out of town. No Beths either, but she may have remarried.

Rivka's next step was to go to the Reading city directories and look for any male siblings since females had probably married with different last names.

Although she had no idea of birth dates, she was aided by knowing the parents' names. She started with the 1921 directory and luckily found three siblings, Allen, William, and Throckton. Assuming and hoping that Throckton was male, she would concentrate on that name since it was so unusual.

She then went to military records and was thrilled to find Second Lieutenant Throckton Ratchford from Reading in January 1940. Records showed that he had married Elizabeth Brookings in 1937 and their residence was London. Checking that phone directory, she crossed her fingers, hoping that they still lived there. Damn it. No Throckton Ratchford in London, although there were three Elizabeths and one E.

She called all four numbers, one of which had been disconnected. The others had no knowledge of Throckton. She was about ready to give up when she checked the 1950 London city directory. Voila! There she found Throckton, his wife Elizabeth B., and one son, Randolph II. Now she was on a roll. Rivka checked the London telephone directory once again, but this time for Randolph II.

It was early evening when she called. A woman answered. Rivka replied that she was trying to find a wartime friend that she believed to be Randolph's aunt. Randolph came on the phone and asked, "Who is it that you are looking for?"

"Throckton's sister, Lillian."

"And how do you know my aunt?"

Excitedly, Rivka replied. "We worked together at Bletchley during the war. My name then was Rivka Schoenstein. It's now Levinson, and we live in the U.S."

"Interesting! So you were one of those code-breakers with Aunt Lillian?"

"Yes. Do you know where I can reach her?"

"Surely. Her name is now Lily Browning, and she lives in Surrey. Give me a couple of minutes and I will get you her address and phone number."

Chapter Eight

She anxiously dialed the number. "Hello."

"Hello. Is this Lillian?"

"This is Lily. Who is this?"

"Lillian, this is Rivka Schoenstein from the days at Bletchley Park."

"My God, Rivka! It is great to hear your voice, but how in the hell did you find me?"

"Just a little detective work, like old times."

"Where are you?"

"I'm in London, close to the Waterloo rail station."

"That's great. You're only about thirty minutes away with lots of departure times. Just hop on one of those trains after you call again to tell me when you will be arriving and I will meet you at the Surrey train station."

An hour and a half later, Rivka was in Surrey, and was one of the first to get off. The two old friends spied one another at the same time and came running toward each other. As they hugged, a man interrupted. "Pardon me, madam. Is this your suitcase?"

"Indeed it is. Thank you, sir."

After the two complimented each other on their looks, Lillian asked if Rivka had eaten.

"Not since breakfast."

"Excellent. There's an excellent Indian restaurant a couple of blocks from here. We can enjoy a leisurely dinner and do a lot of catching up."

"Sounds good. It's been quite a while since I've had a decent Indian meal."

"I recall that you really loved Indian cuisine."

"I still do, but our city lacks a good Indian restaurant." On the way to the restaurant, Lillian said, "You have me curious. You alluded to detective work, but I'm still astounded that you were able to find me."

"Throckton was the key."

"How? He's been dead for at least five years."

"Well, think back to our days at Bletchley. How were we going to break the Nazi code? We had the Enigma, but there was still work to do."

"We worked from what we knew and looked for patterns."

"Exactly. In this case, family ties were the pattern. When I learned that you had a brother named Throckton, I concentrated on him, because of his unusual name. I had to go back to the '50 London city directory but found his son, Randolph II."

"I'm impressed."

"Come on, Lillian. That was simple compared to what we did during the war."

"Well, I can see that you haven't lost your skill."

"Thanks. I'm sure you haven't either, which brings me to why I am here."

Over dinner, Rivka then told her about Alex and all of the "coincidences." When she had finished, Lillian responded. "Rivka, you are right. Too many coincidences. Alex has to be your son."

"Thanks, Lillian, but how do we prove it?"

"You are correct that the orphanage can be expected to push back against any requests for personal information about any of the orphans. So we will have to do what we did against the Nazis when they placed obstacles in our way."

"I figured that you might have an idea or two."

"As a matter of fact, I do. A friend of mine works as a reporter, and her specialty is human interest stories."

"Good morning. This is St. Mary's Orphanage of Wembley."

"Good morning to you. May I speak to your director?"

"Of course. Let me transfer you."

"Thank you."

The Game

A couple of minutes later, she answered. "Good morning, this is Sister Gloria. How may I help you?"

"Good morning, Sister. My name is Marian Stockwell. I'm a reporter for the London Gazette, and I'm writing a human interest story about the orphanages of London during the war. I realize that you are very busy, but if you could find the time for a short interview, I would very much appreciate it."

"Certainly. It sounds interesting. When would be convenient?"

"Early this afternoon, for no longer than an hour, if it works for you."

"Fine. Let's make it at 1:00 p.m."

That evening, at Lillian's invitation, Marian came to dinner at her house to meet Rivka and share what Sister Gloria had told her. After introductions, Marian began. "Lillian, first, let me thank you for putting me on a heartwarming story of courage and sacrifice under unbelievable horror that I'm sure will excite my readers.

"On September 1, 1939, the day of the Nazi blitzkrieg of Poland, there began a mass evacuation of children from London and other large cities or industrial towns that were considered to be potential bombing targets. The evacuations were strictly voluntary, but thousands of parents sent their children off to live in the country either with relatives, or in many cases, with strangers, where they were thought to be safe. This was the first wave, which was followed by a much stronger wave of evacuations a year later when the actual bombing began. However, many of the orphanages on the outskirts of London, including the Wembley orphanage that I visited, did not participate in the evacuations, since it was felt that the children would be much more vulnerable to attack on the roads. Sadly, that turned out to be a deadly mistake.

"Sister Gloria's orphanage was hit by an incendiary bomb at just after 6:00 P.M. on September 12, 1940. There was a massive fire with nineteen fatalities, including three nuns that died trying to save the infants. That more didn't die from the inferno was due to a combination of luck and remarkable heroism.

"The structure was a two-story building, housing ninety-eight children, ranging in age from one to seventeen. There were twelve nuns, three of which were attending to seven toddlers. Fortunately, the bomb hit at dinner time so that all of the children, except the youngest seven, were on the first floor. There was only one stair case, leading from the front door foyer, and that was quickly engulfed in flames. Without any concern for her own safety, a seventeen-year-old girl dashed up the stairs and successfully brought down the youngest and lightest of the babies, a boy just thirteen months old. She, along with the nuns, had wrapped the child in a wet blanket, and she emerged from the building with severe burns on her legs but the baby unharmed. She laid the boy on the ground and tried to go back in, but was restrained by one of the nuns. 'You saved this boy's life. He needs you now.'

"The story ends sadly. All the other babies died in the fire, along with the three nuns. Nine other children succumbed from smoke inhalation."

In tears, Rivka asked, "Did Sister Gloria know what happened to the boy?"

"That night was pandemonium with the surviving nuns trying to restore calm while administering first aid to those in most need. When daylight came, there was an accounting of those who had perished and the survivors, but the girl and the infant were nowhere to be found. The Red Cross had been busy throughout the night and finally arrived about 9:00 a.m. A couple of ambulances carried the most severely burnt victims to nearby hospitals, and other ambulances carried children to orphanages in villages outside London since the Wembley structure was uninhabitable. Even if it had been habitable, remaining in London was no longer a viable option."

"Thanks again, Lillian. You will be reading my story in coming weeks as I visit other orphanages in the area."

"You're welcome, Marian. We'll be looking forward to your story."

As soon as she left, Rivka burst out in tears. "That was my son."

"Yes, I'm sure. Now, all we need to do is find that girl."

After getting the Wembley orphanage phone number from information the next morning, Lillian called and asked to speak to Sister Gloria. Lillian lied, saying that she was a colleague of Marian's at the paper and was following up on the story. "Do you happen to remember the name of the girl who had saved that infant?"

"All I know is that her first name is Allison, the same as my mother's maiden name."

"I see and I assume that you have no idea of her whereabouts or the name of the baby."

"Your assumption is correct."

"Thank you very much."

When Lillian hung up, Rivka asked, "So what now?"

"You had said that Alex was adopted at an orphanage in Middleton Chesney?"

"Yes, but..."

"No buts allowed. I know what you're thinking. They won't tell us anything about Alex, and all we have is the girl's first name."

"Correct."

"So we'll have to improvise. Let's put our Bletchley Park hats on and come up with a plan."

A couple of hours later, after deciding to invent a last name for Allison, Lillian phoned the orphanage.

"Good morning, this is Amazing Grace Children's Home of Middleton Chesney. How may I direct your call?"

"And a good morning to you. May I speak to your director?"

"May I advise her the nature of your business?"

"Certainly. It involves a considerable inheritance."

"Thank you, I will put her on."

"Hello, this is Margaret Finley, and how may I help you?"

"Hello, Ms. Finley. This is Lily Browning, and I have reason to believe that a woman named Allison Frazier left a baby at your orphanage twenty years ago."

"I'm sorry, but we do not give out any information on our children."

"I understand that. I am not wanting information on any of your orphans. It's Ms. Frazier that I'm interested in."

"I'm sorry. That is confidential information."

"This woman's grandfather recently passed away leaving her a considerable amount of money. She is the sole survivor, and if she isn't found, the money will go to the state."

"I see. I will check, but that name doesn't ring a bell."

"That was her birth name. She might have been using the father's name. Were you here during the first bombing raids of the war?"

"Oh yes. I've been here for over twenty-five years and in my current position since April 1940."

"The dates that I would be interested in are September 12, 1940, and up to a few days beyond."

"I'm glad that you have a very narrow time window in mind. That will make it much easier. If you can hold on for a few minutes, I will see what I can find."

"Thank you so much."

Rivka had gone outside when Lillian placed the call because she couldn't bear the suspense. While Lillian was waiting, she was wildly gesturing at the window, but Rivka had her back turned.

The director returned to the phone. "Ms. Browning, I couldn't find anything on Ms. Frazier, but I did see that a Ms. Bankcroft came to our facility on the morning of September 13, 1940 with a one-year-old baby boy. She had been badly burned and asked if she could leave him for a few days while she went to the hospital to be treated. She collapsed as she handed the boy over. We got her to the hospital as soon as we could, but never heard back from her. A

The Game

week had passed when we called the hospital to check on her, but she had died."

"I assume that none of Ms. Bankcroft's family ever came to claim the child."

"That is correct, but now we are getting into confidential information."

"I understand, and thank you for your time."

Lillian called Rivka back into her house and filled her in on the details. As she did, both of them had tears in their eyes. "Thank you, Lillian. I would love to have met that brave woman who saved my son, but at least I know now for sure. I suppose I need to be making plans to get back to my family, but I hope that you will come visit in the not-too-distant future."

"I will, but you're leaving so soon? Aren't you interested in finding your rapist?"

"Do you think he might be in England?"

"I have no idea where he is or if he is even alive, but wouldn't you like to know?"

"Of course, but how?"

"I think you told me that he was a lieutenant colonel in 1938 when he raped you."

"Correct."

"That means that if he survived the war, he was probably at least a colonel. Chances are that that kind of man would have committed war crimes in addition to what he did to you. And if captured, he would have been tried in the Nuremberg trials. Let's see first if he shows up in the register. Surely you remember his name."

"How could I forget?"

An hour later, they were at the library. As a professional genealogist, Lillian didn't even have to ask the location of the World War II archives. After a few minutes, she was able to pull up the record.

Oberst (Colonel) Heinrich Stahl, commandant of Dachau Concentration Camp from March 1942 to April 1945. Disappeared prior to the Allies liberating the camp. Indicted by the Nuremberg Court for crimes against humanity, involving the murder of thousands of inmates, subjecting survivors to torture, medical experiments, and atrocious hygiene conditions, resulting in hundreds more of deaths and permanent disability.

There had been an update on wanted war criminals on December 31, 1959. As of that date, Stahl remained at large.

"So where does that leave us, Lillian?"

"He's probably still alive and if so, almost certainly hiding somewhere in an assumed identity. I think we should start by talking to some of the survivors of Dachau."

Rivka had stopped trying to anticipate the next move. Lillian was on a mission now. Rivka would just sit back and enjoy the ride.

Lillian was back in the microfilm files now. "It says here that there were 30,000 survivors at Dachau when Allied troops liberated the camp on April 29, 1945..."

"Thirty thousand?"

"Yes. But they were described as barely living skeletons. A few were walking, but most were too weak to stand. All who could were singing the praises of their American liberators."

Rivka violated her decision to sit back without questioning. "Thirty thousand survivors? We'll be long dead before we even find most of them, let alone interview them."

"Hush now, Riv. How many do you think are alive today, fifteen years later, after being found in such horrendous conditions?"

"Not many, but how do we find those who are still alive?"

"One step at a time. Let me call Marian and put her on another story."

Marian thanked Lillian, but told her she was covered up with the orphanage story. She gave her the name of another reporter,

The Game

Lena Horowitz, who she knew was very interested in anything to do with the Holocaust.

Lillian then called Ms. Horowitz and gave her a brief rundown on the story they were pursuing. She was excited and agreed to meet Lillian and Rivka for dinner at the same Indian restaurant they had eaten at a couple of days earlier.

A few days later, Lena called Lillian to fill her and Rivka in on what she had learned so far. "The story is really getting interesting. Aside from the 30,000 survivors found on April 29, 7,000 were led on a death march three days earlier south to Tegernsee, a resort town in Southern Germany, where several high-ranking Nazis owned homes, including Kommandant Heinrich Stahl. Leading the march out of Dachau were Stahl and six lower ranking SS officers and a hundred or so enlisted guards.

"The Allies intercepted the death march a few miles from the resort where less than two hundred of the inmates were still barely alive. A few of the survivors reported seeing Stahl and other officers having men their size undress and then executing them before running into the woods with the stolen clothes."

Rivka responded, "So Stahl assumed the identity of one of the inmates?"

"It appears so. I had heard that many of the high-ranking Nazis at concentration camps had done exactly that. The first of my articles on this will be published in Sunday's issue of the Gazette, asking anyone who was a survivor at Dachau, or anyone having information from survivors at Dachau, to get in touch with me."

Rivka agreed to hold off on returning home to see if there were any responses to Lena's article in the Gazette. Lena reported back on Monday afternoon that she had been deluged with phone calls about the article. Two or three survivors reported witnessing Stahl and other SS officers executing prisoners, but could not remember names. Several others had no firsthand knowledge but only knew that one or more of their relatives had been at Dachau. She said that she would keep them posted.

"Lillian, I really appreciate your hospitality and all of the help you've given me. It's been great to catch up with you again, but I need to get back to my family. I know now that Alex is my son. I do hope that you will come for a visit soon."

"Indeed I will, Rivka. I've also tremendously enjoyed our reunion. And I will let you know if anything turns up on that bastard. Let's get on the phone and check departure times. I'll drive you to the airport."

"Thank you."

Chapter Nine

Nate was at the gate when Rivka arrived on time at 9:03 the next evening. He kissed her and asked, "How was your flight?"

"Exhausting after a fifteen-plus hour travel time, but otherwise OK."

"So, did you learn anything?"

"I did. I was able to confirm what we had already been thinking." Over the trip home, she related what she and Lillian had been able to learn.

"All very interesting, but the question now is what do you plan to do with the revelation?"

"The very first thing I plan to do is to get some sleep."

"I had hoped that would be the second thing," he said and they both laughed.

The next morning, Nate brought coffee to Rivka, who was still in bed. She awoke. "My, you're an early bird."

"Not really. I just have to get down to the office, but I thought before I left, you could give me some idea of what you plan."

"I think part of it is very simple. We have to tell Marsha, if for no other reason, to head off a possible romantic situation."

"How?"

"I think the only way is lay it all out. She's old enough to be able to understand."

"Should I be here?"

"I think not. Let two girls handle it."

"What about the other thing?"

"The hunt for the SOB?"

"Yes."

"I think that can wait."

"What should I tell Alex?"

"Nothing for now."

Later, when Marsha came down for breakfast, she greeted her mother with a kiss. "We missed you, Mom, but hope you had an enjoyable trip."

"I did, sweetie, thank you. I missed you both as well, but I have something to tell you. It will take some time, so I hope that you don't have plans this morning."

"Nope. But this sounds serious."

"It is." She proceeded to tell her the whole story dating back to that terrible night in November 1938.

At times, Marsha tried to interrupt and ask a question, but Rivka told her to hold her questions to the end. When Rivka had finished, both were in tears. "Mom, I'm so sorry."

"I know, but the happy part is that I've found my son who is your half-brother, and I'm so proud of both of you."

"What should I say to Alex when he next calls?"

"Let your father and me think on that."

"What if he calls before you've decided?"

"Just say nothing about this."

"Is that fair?"

"Sweetie, ask yourself what would be accomplished? It could put him into a tailspin and affect his work. He would probably want to let his parents know, and he would have a lot of questions for me... the answers of which might not be good for him."

"You mean about the rapist?"

"Yes."

"What about Ingrid?"

"Definitely not. Let's keep this a secret. OK?"

"OK."

Chapter Ten

Two days later, Friday evening, Alex picked the two girls up at Marsha's house again. After that first "double date" for the concert two weeks ago, Alex had taken the girls out twice to movies. Tonight, would be dinner and dancing, but he had not told them where they were going. When they got in the car, he announced that he had a surprise for them. "Ladies, we are going to Der Lukullischer Genuss. Maybe I'll pick up a few words of German over dinner."

The restaurant was one of the swankier ones in town and had the distinction of all German waiters along with the menus themselves also being in German.

Ingrid and Marsha were practically in unison with, "Wow."

"What's the German word for wow?"

Ingrid replied, "Beeindruckend."

"Such a long word for such a short word?"

Marsha managed to break in. "Germans like long words." They all laughed.

Ingrid said, "This is my father's favorite restaurant."

"Great. You'll introduce me, of course."

"I would, but Friday night is his card night. We'll have to come on a Saturday sometime to catch up with him."

They had just finished eating when Alex said,

"Now, let's see how you ladies do at the polka."

Marsha asked to excuse herself, and Ingrid did as well, following her to the rest room. When they got inside, Ingrid said, "Something's bugging you. What's up?"

"Nothing."

"Marsha, I know better. You've barely said anything over dinner."

"I guess I'm not feeling well."

"I'm sorry, but I don't believe you. I think you're jealous. You think that Alex likes me better than you."

"No, no. That's not it at all."

"Then what is it?"

With tears in her eyes, "Ingrid, you're my best friend, but I just can't tell you."

"Didn't we agree that there would be no secrets between us?"

"Yes, but..."

"Yes, but what?"

"He's...my brother."

"Who's your brother?"

"Alex."

"What?" Ingrid's head tilted and her face wrinkled up like she had smelled a foul odor as she tried to comprehend what Marsha had just said.

"It's true. Mom told me the whole story about being raped. I'll fill you in later, but we need to get back to the table."

"All right, but we need to talk first thing tomorrow morning... and you need to tell me everything."

"I will, but promise me that you won't tell Alex."

"I promise."

When they got back to the table, Alex asked, "Who wants to try it first?"

Marsha replied, "Ingrid, you go and I'll watch."

"OK, but if I fall, don't laugh."

"I won't let you fall."

"So you know the polka?"

"Have confidence. We Yalies know how to wing it."

Ingrid got up and found that her best friend's brother had held back that he knew the polka very well. By the end of the evening, Alex had both girls dancing it with fair proficiency. Marsha was beginning to feel good and proud to have such a talented and sweet brother. She even envisaged being Ingrid's maid of honor at her wedding. They would then not only be best friends but sisters-in-law as well.

The next morning at breakfast, Nate told Rivka that he and Alex would be heading to New Haven again for Yale's third game of the season. He was pleasantly and mildly surprised when Rivka agreed to join them. She had never before been that interested in football, but he understood her newly awakened interest in the game. Nate also asked Marsha, but she declined. She and Ingrid had plans.

After they had all left, Marsha called Ingrid to come to her house. Over a couple of cups of coffee, she revealed the whole story to Ingrid as promised. Ingrid sat in awe as her friend spoke.

When Marsha finished, Ingrid remarked, "That man belongs in hell."

"Absolutely. All the Nazis belong in hell."

"I agree. But the part where your brother was rescued by that brave girl about our age was fascinating. That he's here today is a miracle."

"Absolutely, and there might be even a greater miracle in the future." She told Ingrid about her musing of a wedding where she would be Ingrid's maid of honor.

"Wouldn't that be neat? We would all be related."

"I love it."

"On a different subject, I believe that your father was in a concentration camp?"

"Yes, but he won't talk about it."

"What about your mother?"

"She won't either."

"Was she in the same camp?"

"I don't think so. I'm not even sure that she was in a camp, but I don't know. Neither of them will say anything."

"You and I are the same age, so you were two when the war ended. What's your earliest memory?"

"It's all very vague. I remember moving around a lot, and I remember being very cold and hungry at times. But the clearest memory is being on that crowded steamship cold and hungry for several days. And then seeing the Statue of Liberty when everyone cheered."

That evening after Nate and Rivka were in bed reminiscing about the day, Rivka said, "Nate, thanks for bringing me along today. I really enjoyed the game."

"Really? Who won?" He laughed.

Rivka smiled. "Yale!"

"What was the score?"

"Now, you're getting technical."

"I know. I enjoyed it also, and the score is irrelevant." They kissed.

Chapter Eleven

For a couple of weeks, Rivka was hoping to hear from Lillian with some news from the Dachau survivors, but when none came, she put it out of her mind.

Finally, a week or so before Thanksgiving, Lillian called. "Riv, I've got some news."

"Tell me."

"You recall the death march a few days before the camp was liberated with the Nazi officers stripping survivors of their clothes?"

"Yes."

"Lena just called me and said that a survivor of that death march saw Stahl take his friend's clothes and as he executed him, laughingly saying, 'Vielen dank, Jude. Meine Name ist nun Jacob Cohen.' Cohen was the name of the survivor's friend."

"Very interesting, but how do we track down Cohen?"

"Patience, my dear. We know that Stahl had a wife and young daughter. I will begin searching steamship passenger logs for Jacob Cohen, wife and daughter. Stay tuned."

The Levinsons had invited Alex to Thanksgiving dinner, which he graciously accepted. Over dinner, he announced that he would like to take the three of them out on Saturday in appreciation of their kindness.

Marsha blurted out, "Surely you'll include Ingrid." After that first night at the German restaurant, the "double dates" had continued, and the girls had kept their secret from Alex.

Nate sternly replied, "Marsha, it's not your place to add guests to an invitation."

"Mr. Levinson, there's no problem. I was going to ask if it would be all right to ask Ingrid to join us. If agreeable, the restaurant will be Der Lukullischer Genuss. The food is excellent, and you might be surprised at how well Marsha does the polka."

Saturday night, Alex picked up the two girls at Marsha's house and the Levinsons followed in their car. "Nate, I know we've never eaten at this restaurant, but from all reports, I would agree with my son's assessment."

"I'll bet you would agree with him even if the reports were bad."

"Are you accusing me of bias?"

"Yes, but from what I've seen of Alex over the last few months, I would tend to agree with him regardless of reports, too."

Over dinner, Rivka thanked Alex. "The cuisine is fantastic. I can't believe that for all the years we've lived in Albany, we had never dined here."

"Well, there are loads of fine restaurants in the area."

"There are, but we will be back to this one." As Rivka finished her sentence, she suppressed a gasp. She was able to signal Nate unobtrusively with a wink. "If you all will excuse me, I need to powder my nose."

A few minutes later, Nate excused himself. He met Rivka as she was coming out of the restroom. "What's this all about?"

"I saw Stahl or whatever he's calling himself over by the door." Nate looked that way, but it was way across the room, and he was unable to see the table Rivka had referred to.

"You're telling me that with all of the other coincidences involving Alex, that Stahl shows up in Albany and at the same restaurant we're at? I think you've maybe been watching too much of *The Twilight Zone*."

"Maybe, but will you humor me? Go to the phone, call this restaurant and ask for Mr. Cohen. If I'm right, Stahl will get up and answer the phone."

"And if you're wrong, what do I get?"

"I'll give you a kiss and admit I was wrong."

"That's all?"

"Come on, Nate. This is important to me."

Nate went to the pay phone next to the restrooms.

The Game

After dialing information, he called the restaurant."

"Guten abend, good evening. This is Der Lukullischer Genuss. How may I assist you?"

"You have a guest by the name of Cohen. Can you page him please?"

"I am sorry sir, but…"

"This is an emergency, damn it. Page Mr. Cohen!"

"Jawohl, I mean, yes sir!"

Fortunately, the band had not started playing, and the page could be heard clearly throughout the dining room. "Paging Herr Cohen." The page was repeated two minutes later with no response. "Sir, I am sorry, but Mr. Cohen did not answer the page." The line was dead.

Nate laughed. "OK, honey. Payoff time." Rivka blew him a kiss. "You're reneging on the deal, but that's OK. I'll collect tonight."

When they got back to the table, Marsha asked, "Where have you two been? We were ready to send out a search party."

Rivka answered, "Sorry, sweetie. We ran into an old friend and were catching up."

"Well, you're about to meet a new friend. Ingrid spotted her father at a table by the door…"

Rivka paled, "Sweetie, I'm so sorry. Maybe the next time, but your father and I already have made plans with that friend and her husband."

Chapter Twelve

On the drive home from the restaurant, Rivka said, "I knew it. That man was Stahl."

"Goldberg?"

"Yes."

"Honey, you know I love you, but this conspiracy theory is just going too far. You think that Ingrid's father is Stahl?"

"Nate, I realize how bizarre it sounds, and if you believe I need psychiatric help, I don't blame you, but please let me think on this. Perhaps, it's just a case of a person resembling another. If I can't come up with an explanation, I just might agree to see a psychiatrist."

Monday morning, after Nate had left for work and before Marsha got up, Rivka placed a call to Lillian. "Hi Lillian, I hope your reaction is not similar to Nate's..."

She went on to tell her about the incident Saturday night. "Am I crazy, Lillian?"

"No, Riv. There are such things as coincidences. That's why the word exists. Yes, it would be an implausible coincidence added to all the other coincidences with Alex, but I'm not ready to rule it out. One thing tells me that Stahl is not going by the name of Jacob Cohen."

"What is that?"

"Think about it. Would Stahl be so stupid as to announce his new identity to those survivors?"

"You got it, Lillian! Why hadn't I thought about that?"

"Don't be so hard on yourself. You're right in the middle of this, and often one gets a better view of things from the outside. Can you get a photograph of Goldberg?"

"That shouldn't be too difficult. Do you think you can find a photograph of Stahl?"

"I think so. Let me get to checking, and how about if we talk again in a couple of days?"

"That sounds good, but let's keep our phone conversations about this time of day. Right now, I'd rather keep this from Nate and Marsha."

"I understand."

Three days later, at about the same time, the phone rang, and Rivka picked it up quickly. "Hello."

"Hi Riv. It's Lillian."

"I thought it might be you, but unfortunately I haven't been able to find a single photo of Goldberg."

"No problem, Riv. I decided to get some information on him."

"I'm listening."

"There were fourteen survivors from Dachau named Goldberg. I found annual logs of inmates from '41 through '44. Over a hundred Goldbergs in all that we can assume perished."

"What's that get us?"

"We'll focus first on the shorter list. Do you know your Goldberg's first name?"

"That should be a lot easier than the photo, but please don't refer to him as my Goldberg."

Lillian chuckled, "OK, we'll call him the Albany Goldberg. As soon as you get his first name, give me a call."

A few minutes later, Rivka returned the call. "That was quick."

"It was a lot easier than searching for a photograph. I just called the library to get the faculty register for the high school. German teacher, Haim Goldberg."

"Good, Riv. Hold on a second." Rivka waited anxiously until Lillian came back on the line. "No Goldberg survivors shown as Haim. Let me go through the other lists. Fortunately, they are alphabetized... Here it is. Haim Goldberg: 1941, 1942, 1943."

Rivka couldn't wait until Nate got home from work and hoped that Marsha would be out when he arrived. She was thinking about the phone call when she heard her daughter coming down the stairs. "Good morning, sweetie. Coffee is ready and I'll have your breakfast ready in a few minutes."

"Thanks, Mom."

"Any plans today?"

"Just going to putter around till 4:45. Alex will be picking me and Ingrid up for dinner and a movie."

Perfect. "On a Thursday night? And so early?"

"Yes. He and Dad are headed to a night basketball game in New Haven tomorrow, and also it's a work day for Alex."

"Oh, yes. I understand, and I had forgotten about the ball game."

That evening after Marsha had left and Nate arrived, she greeted him at the door with a hug and a kiss. "Wow! What's that for? Not that I have any problem with that."

"I have wonderful news."

He laughed, "We're going to have a baby?"

"No, silly. Mr. Goldberg is not Goldberg. He's Stahl."

"I thought you had put that thought in the wastebasket where it belongs."

"Just sit down and listen." Rivka related her phone call with Lillian. "The prisoner log at Dachau shows that Haim Goldberg was there in '41, '42 and '43, but he does not show up in the '44 logs."

"So?"

"So? So, Goldberg must have died before the '44 count was taken."

"Honey, you are not being logical. You're leaving out the possibilities of his escape or being transferred."

"What's the probability of escaping from one of those camps, and why would they choose to transfer a prisoner?"

"I don't know, but you haven't proved a thin-"

"Wait! I've got it."

"Got what?"

The Game

"How old is Ingrid?"

"Am I supposed to know that? And what does that have to do with the subject at hand?"

"We both know that Ingrid is about Marsha's age, and if that is so, how could Ingrid be Goldberg's daughter?"

"First, we don't know when that count was taken. Very possibly early 1943, and if Goldberg escaped after that date, Ingrid could have been born in late 1943 and be just a few months younger than Marsha. Second, we don't know Ingrid's age. We are only assuming that they're about the same age. And, lastly, Ingrid might have been adopted. Too many loopholes for me."

"You're impossible!"

The next morning, same time, Rivka called Lillian.

"Hello."

"Hi Lillian. Nate's not buying it." She related his objections. "He keeps throwing up roadblocks."

"OK, let me do some more checking, and I'll get back to you."

"All right. I'll be on pins and needles, but let's wait till Monday morning, same time."

"Sure thing!"

The phone rang at the appointed time, and Rivka excitedly answered. "Hello!"

"Hi. I've got some information."

"Go on. I've got pencil and paper."

"Haim Goldberg and his wife, Ruth, and their daughter entered the U.S. at Ellis Island on August 10, 1950. His declared place and date of birth as well as Ruth's match the hospital records..."

"Yes, but what about Ingrid?"

"Very good question. He stated that she was born in Hamburg on April 23, 1943..."

"And?"

"And no record of any Ingrid Goldberg at any Hamburg hospital on that date..."

"Could he have been a few days off?"

"I considered that possibility, and the answer is no. No Ingrid Goldberg for March, April, or May."

"Fantastic, but I can anticipate Nate's response. He will say that it doesn't prove Goldberg was lying. He might just have been confused on the date or the city."

"Well, if he was only confused on the city, Ingrid would be the shortest-term baby ever since we know from the log that Goldberg was a prisoner at the very least until January 1, 1943."

"Great work, Lillian. By the way, did you ever find a photograph of Stahl?"

"Actually, I have several that I can send you."

"Thank you, Lillian."

"My pleasure."

An hour or so later, Marsha came down stairs. "Good morning, Mom."

"Good morning, sweetie. I'll get some breakfast going. How'd you sleep?"

"Fine. I'm just wondering."

"Wondering what, honey?"

"When are we going to tell Alex?"

"I'm not sure."

"Mom, we have to tell him. It's not fair."

"I know, sweetie, but it's complicated."

"How so?"

"Let me talk to your father tonight."

"Can't I be part of the discussion?"

"I suppose so."

That evening at dinner, Rivka broached the subject. "Nate, Marsha asked if we could tell Alex..."

"I would rather not."

"Why Dad? And please don't tell me it's complicated."

"Honey, what would be gained?"

"Don't you think he would want to know?"

"Possibly, but we don't know what his reaction would be. He has brought on several new clients and in a short time has established himself as an indispensable part of my business."

"So, it's all about business! It's just not fair!" Marsha was crying as she left the dinner table with most of her food uneaten.

"Sweetie, come on back and finish your meal. I will talk to your dad tonight."

In bed, Rivka brought up the subject again. "Nate, she has a point, and I've learned some more about Goldberg. He was lying when they entered the U.S. through Ellis Island." She filled him in with the latest information from Lillian.

"What if she was adopted? Her birth name wouldn't have been Goldberg at birth."

"You just don't want to believe."

"Honey, you know that's not true. What you're suggesting is so bizarre, and you haven't proved your case."

"OK. Lillian will be sending some photos of Stahl, but what about Alex?"

"If what you're saying about Goldberg is true, not that I am even beginning to believe it, but if it is true, that presents a whole other set of problems."

"So what do I tell Marsha?"

"Just try to put it off, at least till we're able to prove or disprove your wild suspicion."

The next morning at breakfast, Marsha asked, "Mom, did you have a chance to talk to Dad about Alex?"

"Yes, and he would prefer to put it off for now."

"That sounds like forever."

"No, sweetie." Now she was lying. "If he really is my son, we all need to know."

"What do you mean 'if'? I thought the story you told me proved it."

"I know, but that's what I was referring to when I said there are complications. Lillian has come up with some additional information that she will be sending in a letter."

"Why a letter? Couldn't she just have told you over the phone?"

"No, it involves photographs."

"Geez, this is getting weirder and weirder. First, he's your son and my brother, and now you're not sure?"

"Let's just wait and see."

"What'll I tell Ingrid?"

"Nothing for now, but since you brought up Ingrid, was she adopted?"

"Mom, this conversation is getting crazier by the minute. What does that have to do with what we were talking about?"

"Nothing, really, but it just seemed odd that both Alex and Ingrid were orphans."

"Whatever gave you the idea that Ingrid was adopted?"

"Something that Alex said. Perhaps I misunderstood."

"Well, I don't know what Alex might have said, but I can assure you that Ingrid is Goldberg's daughter by birth. All you have to do is look at the two of them. She actually looks more like him than her mother."

Rivka thought to herself before responding, And she also looks a lot like Alex. "So you got to meet them at the German restaurant?"

"You forget, Mr. Goldberg is my German teacher."

"Oh yes, I forgot."

"But, yes. I got to meet her mother when we were all introduced. You and Dad didn't miss much in not meeting them."

"You weren't impressed?"

"Not terribly. Mrs. Goldberg is OK, I guess, but seems pretty meek. Mr. Goldberg has no personality, whatsoever."

"I gather that you don't like him too much."

"Ha. Too much is an understatement. I can't stand him, and that goes for most of the class. But I'm learning German, and that's the important thing."

"So he's a good teacher?"

"I suppose."

"All right honey, let's wait for that mail, and then we can decide."

Three days later, Rivka got an unexpected call from Lillian. "I had to let you know what I found. Ruth Goldberg did not show up in Dachau at all..."

"Meaning that she was transported to another camp, which would have been unlikely since they normally sent couples to the same place, or that she escaped capture."

"Exactly. Haim Goldberg was arrested on May 3, 1941, so I looked for Ruth Goldberg immigrating to England or to the U.S. in that time frame. I found that Ruth Goldberg came through Ellis Island on June 10, 1941."

"Haim Goldberg's wife?"

"Yes. The correct birth date and place, and her declaration states married to Haim Goldberg."

"Were you able to trace her from there?"

"Yes, she moved to Chicago to live with a Shapiro family related to her mother. She passed away on January 11, 1953 and is buried at Oak Woods Cemetery."

Chapter Thirteen

Finally, that night, after Rivka filled him in on the latest from Lillian, Nate believed what she had been telling him. He didn't even need the part about Marsha stating that Ingrid looked more like her father than her mother. Nate had apparently repressed it, but now acknowledged the resemblance between Alex and Ingrid.

"The question, now is how do we exact justice on this SOB?"

"Good question, Nate. I'm hoping that you can come up with an answer."

"Let's sleep on it, and maybe something will come to me in a dream."

The next morning at breakfast, Nate was still trying to come up with a plan. "One thing for sure is that we can't let the cat out of the bag. If Stahl realizes we're on to him, he could disappear and we would never find him."

"I understand."

"I've decided to fill Alex in totally. I'll ask him to come to the office tomorrow morning for an urgent matter. Being Saturday, there won't be any interruptions."

"OK. I will let Marsha know..."

"Only that he is your son and Marsha's brother."

"Of course."

When Marsha came down to eat, Rivka said, "Your father has decided to tell Alex tomorrow morning, but mum's the word till then."

"That's great, and I won't say a word."

"Not even to Ingrid. One day won't make any difference when all three of you will know."

The next morning, Alex was at the office at 9:00, as requested. "Good morning, Mr. Levinson."

"Good morning, Alex. Care for some coffee? It's ready, and there are some doughnuts."

"Think I will, and thanks."

"Thank you for coming in on a Saturday. I would like to tell you how impressed I am with your performance over the last several months. You have more than earned your keep, and I'm giving you a 15% raise starting Monday."

"That's great, sir, and I appreciate it."

"No thanks needed. You earned it. Now another matter that I would like to discuss with you in strictest confidence."

"Of course."

"I have to warn you. This news will shock you and make you angry, but please bear with me."

Alex's countenance morphed from a grin to a somber look. "Certainly, sir."

Nate began with a similar somber look, "Alex, your mother..." Alex's eyes widened. "Was raped as a girl in Germany."

"Oh, my God!"

"And that girl was...Mrs. Levinson."

"My mother? Mrs. Levinson?"

"Yes. As I told you, this would come as a shock." Nate continued to tell him the whole story of Rivka coming to England on the Kindertransport in December 1938, and placing Alex in the orphanage at Wembley, and the remarkable rescue by that girl and his transfer to Middleton Chesney.

When Nate had finished with Alex's background, Alex remarked, "We need to find that bastard and string him up by his balls."

"Pleasant thought, Alex, but that brings me to the rest of the story. We know where he is, but we need to be extremely cautious in handling the situation. If he has any inkling that we're on to him, he may disappear, and our hopes of extracting justice will disappear along with him. You've met the man... His name is Haim Goldberg."

Incredulous, Alex responded, "Ingrid's father?"

"Yes. I had a hard time believing it until Rivka laid out the facts." He then related the entire story about Stahl at Dachau, entering the U.S as Goldberg, his wife and daughter, and the clincher about Ruth Goldberg.

When he had finished, Alex commented, "That is all incredible and so much to digest, but I have to say that you've done your homework."

"Not I, Alex. It was your mother and her friend from England."

"OK. So, what do I call you now, Pop or Dad?"

"Neither. Your father is in Boston. I'm just the fellow that was lucky enough to marry your mother. But you can dispense with the Mr. Levinson. Just call me Nate."

"Well, Nate, what do we do now?"

"We have to plan very carefully. We dare not let this information get to Ingrid or Marsha, for that matter. If Marsha knows, she could inadvertently let it slip. And then as I said earlier, Stahl could be gone in a flash, leaving us little opportunity to ever catch up with him."

"Well, here's some information that I think might be helpful. Ingrid despises her father and has considered running away, but she fears for her mother's safety. When he drinks, which is frequently, he can go into a rage at the slightest provocation and beat his wife relentlessly."

"That's some good information. Perhaps Ingrid and her mother could be allies at a later date, but we still can't risk Stahl knowing that we are on to him."

"So, where do we go from here?"

"I've been mulling it around. We have an isolated cabin in the mountains not far from here. We haven't used it for a few years, and it is in terrible disrepair, but for our purposes, it should be fine. I don't have the details yet, but I think we will need to abduct Goldberg and force him to reveal his true identity."

"Is there any question?"

"From what we know, I'm one hundred percent certain that he is a Nazi. I'm 95% sure that he is Stahl, but I would like to make absolutely sure. Besides, whether he is Stahl or just another Nazi, I think he deserves some special treatment." Nate laughed and Alex joined in.

"Let's continue to refer to him as Goldberg, even among ourselves. I don't want it to inadvertently slip and let him know that we are on to him. This will be important when we turn him over to law enforcement. We can't be asking any leading questions."

"What about his Fifth Amendment rights?"

"We won't have to ask him about any of his atrocities. That can come out at trial."

"All we want to do is to get him to admit who he is without giving him any idea what we know, except that he is not Goldberg and that we suspect him of being a Nazi."

"Isn't that a violation of the Fifth Amendment?"

"It would be if we were to try to use the confession. The information we already have should be enough to establish his true identity. But what you told me about his wife gives me an additional idea. Let's start thinking about how we might kidnap Goldberg. How about getting together again at 8:00 a.m. on Monday? That will give us plenty of time to discuss before the market opens."

"Sounds good. I have another double date with the girls tonight. I will try to glean a little information from Ingrid that may help."

"Just be unobtrusive."

"Of course."

That evening, Alex and the girls were in the middle of their meal at the German restaurant when Alex spotted Goldberg and his wife entering, "Ingrid, I see your mom and dad just coming in.

Why don't you ask them to join us? We can scoot around and make room."

"Are you sure about that?"

"Absolutely." Ingrid had misgivings, but thought that it might not be a bad idea for Alex to get better acquainted with her folks if Marsha's musing turned out to actually happen. She left their table and greeted her parents. Goldberg appeared to be reluctant but acquiesced at his wife's urging.

"Guten Abend, Herr und Frau Goldberg."

Goldberg smiled and replied, "Guten abend. So, sprichst du Deutsch?"

"No sir. Ingrid and Marsha have been trying to teach me, however I'm not a very good student."

"Ha, perhaps you need a better teacher."

"Perhaps. Marsha has told me what a good teacher you are."

"I don't delude myself into thinking that the students like me. I am harsh and demanding, but to learn anything, it takes discipline and hard work. It took me years to learn to speak English correctly."

"And you do so very well. On a different subject, Ingrid has told me that you are a card player. Are you as good at cards as you are at English?"

"I think that I am. Are you a card player also?"

"Yes sir. And I'm a lot better at cards than in speaking German."

The band had begun playing, and Ingrid seized the opportunity to break into the conversation. "Alex, let's dance, and you can show my parents that you are also pretty good at the polka."

"Girl, can't you see I am having a conversation with Alex?"

Ingrid snapped back, "Father, can't you see that there are other people at the table? Come on, Alex."

"Excuse us, sir and ladies." He took Ingrid's hand and led her to the dance floor.

The Game

Goldberg's face reddened. "The impudence of that girl." Ruth and Marsha smiled.

"What are you two smiling about?"

On the dance floor, Ingrid said, "Alex, I don't think it was such a good idea to invite them to our table."

"I'm sorry. I just wanted to get to know your folks better."

"I see. Tell me what you now know about my mother that you didn't know earlier."

"Umm. She's pretty quiet."

"When did she have a chance to say anything?" They both laughed.

When the two returned and before Goldberg was able to say anything, Marsha stood up. "My turn now."

As Marsha and Alex were leaving the table, Goldberg called out, "What games are you proficient in?"

Alex responded over his shoulder. "You name the game – gin rummy, poker, euchre..."

When Alex and Marsha returned to the table, he started to ask Mrs. Goldberg for the next dance but was loudly interrupted by her husband. "No! Sit! Poker and gin rummy?"

"Yes, sir. Mind you, sir, only modest stakes."

"What do you mean by modest?"

"In college, we played gin for a penny a point, and poker a quarter ante with a dollar maximum raise."

"Ha. Childish stakes. What stakes do you play in now?"

"I haven't played since college. What are your stakes?"

"Twenty-five cents for gin and dollar ante for poker with table stakes."

"Beeindruckend!"

"I think that you are being modest about your German."

"Not at all. That's a word that your daughter taught me. Your stakes at poker would probably have me wiped out in less than an hour, but I would like to give gin a try if you would be kind enough to humor me. I will warn you. I'm pretty good."

"Be at our house tomorrow at 8:00 p.m. and bring some money. Ingrid can give you directions."

"Thank you, Mr. Goldberg. I will be looking forward to it."

"I too. By the way, I see that you are pretty proficient in the polka. We'll see if your skill at gin matches that of your dancing."

"We shall see." He gestured toward Mrs. Goldberg. "May I?"

She smiled. "I would be delighted."

On the dance floor, Alex remarked, "You dance beautifully. Do you and Mr. Goldberg dance much?"

"We used to, but now he prefers to talk and drink."

"And play cards?"

"Yes, and be careful. He's very good."

"I'm not bad."

When they returned, Goldberg surprised them all and led his wife back to the dance floor. While they were dancing, Ingrid said that she had a headache and wanted to leave.

Alex signaled the waiter for his share of the bill and said, "Let's wait till they get back, and we'll excuse ourselves."

Alex had paid his bill when the Goldbergs returned. "You two dance very well together. We would love to stay a bit longer, but Ingrid has a headache, so we will be saying, aufwiedersehen."

"Aufwiedersehen, Alex, and don't forget 8:00 p.m. tomorrow."

"I won't."

As they were leaving the restaurant, Ingrid spoke, "Alex and Marsha, I apologize for my father. He can be pretty abusive."

Alex responded with a lie. "Oh, he's not that bad. So where to now? Do you really have a headache?"

"Amazingly, it's gone. How about some rock and roll?"

"I know just the place," Marsha responded and gave Alex directions.

The next night, precisely at 8:00 p.m., Alex knocked on the Goldberg door.

"Welcome, Alex. You are right on time."

The Game

"I try to be, sir."

Ingrid had wanted to sit and watch, but Goldberg made it clear that there would be no spectators except for Mrs. Goldberg to keep them supplied in beer or liquor and pretzels.

"So, Alex Greenbaum. Jew or German?"

"Neither, sir. I was adopted. My adoptive father is Jewish and mother is Protestant. I was baptized as a Methodist."

Goldberg smiled. "I see."

They sat down at the card table, and Goldberg laid out the rules. "Twenty-five cents a point, one hundred points to the game, a bonus of twenty points for a game, twenty-five points for gin or under-cut on a knock and double for a blitz. I hope you are prepared with money."

"I think I have enough, sir."

Goldberg smirked. *I'll have this whippersnapper cleaned out and begging for mercy in an hour.*

Thirty minutes later, with Alex nursing his second beer and Goldberg on his second vodka tonic, Alex led in the first game, 72 to 19. The next hand, after two draws, Alex knocked with six. He caught Goldberg with several picture cards of deadwood and only two cards that he could play off on Alex's hand. Final score on the first game with the twenty-point bonus was 143 to 19. Alex was off to a good start, up $31.00.

Goldberg was not happy, but was convinced that first game was all luck. Alex had just gotten the cards. He had finished his third drink and Alex was on his third beer. "Alex, drink up. You will join me in Schnapps, and we will change the rules. Are you familiar with Hollywood scoring?"

"Yes, sir, but that can get pretty expensive."

"Alex, you're way ahead. Are you afraid to go Hollywood?"

"No sir. But just to make sure that I understand the rules. Same stakes as before, but this time we will be scoring three games concurrently. The score of the first hand goes on the first game. If the winner of the second hand is the same as the winner of the first hand, his score is entered on both games. And likewise, until the loser of a previous hand wins a hand, he receives no score in any of the games, so blitzes become more prevalent. This is what makes the game potentially so expensive."

"You understand correctly." Goldberg shuffled the cards and asked Alex to cut.

The first hand, Goldberg quickly knocked with eight, catching Alex with twenty-two. The next hand, Alex knocked with three, catching Goldberg with seventeen of deadwood. Several hands later, after two gins and an undercut, the score was 111 to 14 in the first game, 102 to zero in the second game for a blitz, and Alex at 78 in the third game with another potential blitz. Alex quickly knocked, catching Goldberg with a pile. When the accounting for the bonuses was done, Alex had won the three games by 586 points or $146.50. That added to his previous $31 made for a pretty nice evening's work.

"Let's have one more drink and one final game for double stakes."

"I am sorry, Mr. Goldberg. I hate to leave with my winnings, but if I have another drop of alcohol, I won't be able to make it home."

"All right, Alex. Let's see if you're as good at poker as you are at gin. Join us next Friday for a game at a friend's house. The game starts at 7:00 p.m. I will pick you up at 6:30."

"Thank you, sir, but the least I can do after your hospitality is use my car and my gas. I will pick you up at 6:30."

Chapter Fourteen

Monday morning at 8:00, Alex met Nate at his office as planned. Alex filled Nate in on the weekend's events and the scheduled card game Friday night. For the next hour and a half, plans were laid, with some adjusting over the next few days.

Friday night, as scheduled, Alex pulled up to Goldberg's house. Goldberg answered the knock quickly and joined Alex in his car. "I hope that you are ready for some real poker tonight. You will need all your winnings from Sunday and then some."

"I'm ready, sir."

When they arrived, Goldberg introduced Alex to the five other players. "Gentlemen, this is my new young friend, Alex Greenbaum. He is quite a good gin rummy player. We will see tonight if he is as skilled at poker." They all laughed, including Alex.

He knew that he was in deep water, but poker was the last thing on his mind. He was thinking about what was planned for the drive after they left the game.

Everyone bought their chips, and Alex laid down his $177.

An hour into the game, Alex was holding his own. He had won a couple of pots and was only down about twenty dollars from where he had started in the evening. With his winnings at gin, he was still over a hundred ahead.

The game ended at 10:30. Alex had been wiped out an hour and a half earlier, but the fun was about to begin. Goldberg and Alex said their farewells and headed to his car. "Well, Alex. You can consider tonight your first tuition payment. You are not a bad poker player, but you have much to learn." Goldberg, despite four vodka tonics, had done quite well. He had recovered his losses from Sunday night's gin and was up over $200. He was a bit woozy by now, and that suited Alex's purposes very well.

Alex, on the other hand, had nursed his second vodka tonic while he watched the game after having dropped out. That he was no longer playing, the players didn't notice or mind that he wasn't drinking along with them. "Thank you, sir. One can never learn enough." He pulled out into the street, sped up, and suddenly swerved to the right, causing Goldberg to lurch to the left. At that moment, Alex injected a dose of midazolam into Goldberg's neck.

"What the hell did you..."

The sedative coupled with the alcohol caused Goldberg to fall off into a deep sleep almost instantly. Alex pulled off at a gas station and called Nate at the cabin. "We're set and should be there in about thirty minutes."

"Great, all ready here. I'll call Rivka and tell her to proceed with the call to Mrs. Goldberg."

After Nate called Rivka, she in turn called Goldberg's house. Ingrid answered and Rivka said, "Hello, Ingrid. May I speak to your mother?"

"Of course. I'll put her on." She called out, "Mom, it's Alex's mother for you."

"Thank you, dear." She picked up. "Hello."

"Hello, Mrs. Goldberg. Please don't be alarmed. Your husband is safe and being detained, pending a release to authorities for impersonation and entering this country illegally."

"So, you know?"

"Yes, we know everything. If you would, please come over with Ingrid tomorrow morning. Marsha will join us, and I will tell all of you the whole story, including what you don't know."

"What time?"

"What time suits?"

"9:00?"

"That will work. I will have coffee and doughnuts ready."

When Goldberg came to, he found himself naked and tied to a heavy oak chair. His arms and legs were tightly bound, and although there was a good fire in the fireplace, the temperature in

The Game

the cabin was pretty low. They had thrown a blanket over him to keep him from dying of hypothermia. "Where are my clothes? I am freezing."

Nate responded, "You'll get them in due time, but right now, we're going to play a little game called Truth or Consequences. Answer correctly and you will be rewarded, but on the other hand..."

"This is insane. This is how you justify stealing my money."

"Not at all. We're not interested in your money. We only want the truth. The game begins. What is your name?"

"I refuse to play your insane game."

"Wrong answer... Alex, proceed with the consequence."

His eyes widened in terror as he watched Alex remove the red-hot poker from the fire and brandish it. Goldberg screamed, and the next thing he knew was the excruciating pain from the poker being rammed into his right ear. His screaming continued as shrill and loud as before, but all at once, it seemed only half as loud to him. "You people are mad."

Alex chuckled, "You may have something there, but you said you were cold. Just warming you up a bit."

Nate asked again, "What is your name?"

The hearing in his right ear was gone, but he was still able to hear the question. Screaming, he responded. "What do you want me to say?"

"Oh, wrong answer again. Alex..."

"No! No!" Goldberg's eyes were bulging almost out of their sockets and his face had lost all color.

Goldberg was crying through his screams as Alex lowered the blanket and pushed the poker like the point of a sword into Goldberg's right nipple, leaving it until there was a hissing sound and some smoke.

Goldberg cursed as he screamed. "You people will go to hell." He strained to move back from the searing heat to no avail.

A minute or so later, Alex pulled the poker away, and Nate said, "Now, let's try again. What is your name?"

"Haim Goldberg, damn it!"

"Sorry, wrong answer... Alex..." Alex was clearly enjoying himself as he again retrieved the poker from the fire and brandished it like the swordfighters of old. "Touché." Alex shoved the poker into Goldberg's navel, twisting it a bit for good measure and leaving it there again long enough for a faint amount of smoke to emit. Goldberg's throat was raw and his voice hoarse from screaming in agony as he tried in vain to back away. He was now sitting in his own pile of excrement and urinating on the floor.

"You are a slow learner, but I'm confident that you will get it right. Again, your name?"

He hesitated as there was a sudden realization on his part. After each wrong answer that poker was lowered and now obviously headed in a dreaded direction. Before Nate could ask again, he responded, "All right, I will tell you, but promise that the torture will cease."

"I will consider your offer. What is your name?"

"Heinrich Stahl."

"Heinrich Stahl? Are you certain?"

"What name do you want?"

"Just your correct name."

"My name is Heinrich Stahl."

"But you entered this country under the assumed name of Haim Goldberg?"

"Yes."

"Are you circumcised?"

"No, damn it. That's only for you damn Jews."

Alex replied, "Watch it Stahl. You might get into trouble."

"I gave you the answer you wanted. Now untie me and give me back my clothes and money."

The Game

"Be patient, Stahl. Alex and I think we need to help you with your problem." Nate uncovered Stahl's genitals. Nate and Alex chuckled.

Stahl grimaced with fear. "You told me that if I answered the question correctly that you would stop this stupid game."

"You must have misunderstood. We told you that if you answered correctly, you would be rewarded. You haven't been circumcised, and we can fix that."

"You can take your circumcised penises and shove them up each other's ass."

"Oh, oh, such disrespect. What do you think, Alex?"

"Nate, I really don't think he is worthy of circumcision. Someone might think he is a Jew." Alex retrieved the red-hot poker and proceeded to Stahl with it.

Stahl was shivering with terror and his eyes looked like they were going to pop out of his head as he comprehended what was coming next. "You cannot do this. This is a war crime."

With that statement, Alex and Nate burst out laughing. "Listen to who is talking about war crimes." Alex continued, "Another benefit of this method is that I won't have any more siblings by this bastard."

The poker was now moving in what appeared to be slow motion as Stahl followed its movement like someone tied to the railroad tracks with a train approaching. As cold as it was, beads of sweat appeared on his forehead. "NO, NO!" he screamed.

His voice at this point was so raw that his screams were barely above a whisper, and then silence as he fainted from fright.

Moments later as he pulled the poker away, Alex remarked, "Stahl, you don't have to worry. Anyone looking at that will never mistake you for a Jew." He was already unconscious, but Alex administered another dose of midazolam for good measure. "Sleep well, Stahl, and we will deliver you to the FBI in the morning fully dressed."

The next morning, over coffee and doughnuts, Rivka revealed the whole story to Ruth, Ingrid, and Marsha. Ingrid and Marsha, of course, knew about Alex, but not the truth about Stahl. Ruth, on the other hand, knew Stahl, but had no idea of the connection to Rivka. When she finished, they all cried.

Ruth, with tears in her eyes, said, "I knew he was an evil man, but I had no idea…"

Rivka responded, "I know, and I too am sorry."

Ruth replied, "No, Rivka. You owe us no apology. It is we who owe you."

Ingrid hugged Marsha's neck, "I am so sorry. I knew that he was a terrible father and husband, but…"

Chapter Fifteen

"Mr. Goldberg, my name is Eugene White with the FBI. You are under arrest for entering the U.S. under a false identity with your wife and daughter. You are also under the suspicion of being a Nazi officer having committed war crimes. You have the right to remain silent. Anything you say may be held against you. You have the right to retain a lawy..."

"Ha, my Fifth Amendment rights have already been violated. The confession they extracted from me was under the duress of torture."

"What confession? They said nothing about a confession. They merely performed a Constitutionally valid act of a citizen's arrest for entering the U.S. illegally and suspicion of being a Nazi war criminal with ample documentation to back up their charge. Now let me finish a recitation of your Miranda rights. You have the right to retain a lawyer."

"Look at what they did to me," he said as he pointed to his ear. "I will show you the burns..."

"Mr. Goldberg, that is all irrelevant. You can press charges for assault if you wish, but right now, I need to know if you understand your Miranda rights."

"Yes, but my rights have already been violated."

"Do you wish to say anything more?"

"Only that I want to call my lawyer."

"Fine. You can tell him or her that you will be transported to Ray Brook Penitentiary to await arraignment within a day or two."

He was escorted to another room without windows, and the FBI agent waited outside while he made the call.

"Fred Evans here."

"Fred, this is Goldberg. I've got a bit of a sticky problem."

"Like what?"

"False identity."

"True or false?"

"They violated my Fifth Amendment rights against self-incrimination."

"So, true?"

"Yes, but..."

"Sounds like an easy case. We get the confession thrown out, and you acknowledge the deception. Maybe get you off with a fine or at most a little jail time."

"There is a complication."

"What's the complication?"

"I can't acknowledge the deception."

"Are you guilty of false identity or not?"

"I'm also being charged as a war criminal."

"Holy Christ, Goldberg! What else haven't you told me?"

"That's it, except for false identity for Ruth and Ingrid."

"So a family affair?" Evans chuckled. "Sorry buddy. If there are any grounds for the war crimes charge, and it appears there are, you need a much higher-powered attorney than me and more than a little help from the Big Guy Above."

"So you're throwing me overboard?"

"I'm being honest with you. If you can tell me why the war crimes charge is bogus, then maybe I can help you."

"The allegations are groundless. I was merely following orders."

"Sorry, buddy. That argument won't work."

A day later, he was brought before the arraignment judge. "Mr. Goldberg, you may stand. The charges against you are entering this country illegally and under a false identity. Also that you have committed war crimes under international law. How do you plead?"

"Not guilty, Your Honor."

"Prosecution, what evidence do you have?"

The Game

The prosecutor approached the bench and handed the judge a packet of papers. "Too much paperwork. Can you tell me succinctly what you have?"

"It's all there, Your Honor, but what may be of most interest is the testimony of my first witness. Mrs. Ruth Goldberg, please come to the stand."

Stahl rose and yelled, "Objection, Your Honor. A wife can't testify against her husband."

The judge asked, "Is Mrs. Ruth Goldberg your wife?"

"Yes. She can't testify against me."

"Objection sustained." Stahl broke into a big smile.

"Sorry, Your Honor. Prosecution then calls Mrs. Heinrich Stahl to the witness stand."

Stahl screamed as he rose, "No! She cannot testify. Objection!"

"What is your objection, Mr. Goldberg?"

"That's the same woman."

"Mrs. Heinrich Stahl is Mrs. Ruth Goldberg?"

"Yes, Your Honor."

"I'm confused. Which is her correct name?"

"Ruth Goldberg, my wife."

"Objection sustained. Counselor, do you have anything else?" Again, Stahl smiled.

"Yes, Your Honor. Sidebar, please?"

"Yes."

The prosecutor approached the bench. "Thank you, Your Honor. There is a question of Mrs. Stahl's identity. I would merely like to establish that she is in fact Mrs. Heinrich Stahl, not Mrs. Ruth Goldberg."

"All right, but no questions regarding any private communication between the two."

"I understand."

"Objection overruled. You may proceed, Mr. Prosecutor."

The prosecutor walked back to the counsel table. "Mrs. Heinrich Stahl, please take the witness chair."

Chapter Sixteen

"The wheels of justice turn slowly, but grind exceedingly fine." Many months later, at the Hague, another Nuremburg war crimes trial was just finishing up. "Colonel Heinrich Stahl, the Court finds you guilty of all charges under the International War Crimes Act. The sentence is death by hanging, which shall be carried out at midnight on November 9, 1961."

Epilogue

You may have thought we were finished with the coincidences, but not quite. As it turns out, a young junior reporter at a local newspaper in Northfield, Indiana, penned the following article, which appeared in the May 8, 1970 issue of the Northfield Informer.

My name is Wendy Levinson Greenbaum, and I am a junior reporter for our daily newspaper. When I was given the assignment to do some research and come up with a human-interest story commemorating the twenty-fifth anniversary of VE Day, I thought it was just another "make-work" project for an inconsequential, inexperienced reporter. How wrong I was. I hope that this story of miracles and heroism will touch you as it has me.

I found this account of a bombing mission by a local hero and the attached letter in our archives. Somehow, it missed publication, but I think it is fitting that it be published on this anniversary of the end of that terrible war. The following account was written by Edward Harrington, a U.S. Air Force captain and pilot of the B-17. I tried to locate him for a personal interview, but learned that he had passed away three years ago. To date, I have not been able to find any surviving family members.

"On April 24, 1944, my B-17 bomber, The Mary Jane, was one of several hundred bombers destined for runs at Munich and heavy industrial areas nearby. Across the channel and into France, we were protected by the P-47 Jugs and P-38 Lightnings. Due to limited range, our protection into Germany and our target, protection depended on the formidable P-51 Mustangs and our own

The Game

limited firepower. Not to denigrate our gunners, but thank God for those magnificent Mustangs.

"As predicted, the Jerries were expecting us with hundreds of Me-109s as well as massive numbers of anti-aircraft positions all along our route. Our particular mission was firebombing Munich. The city was not one of the targets chosen for its military purposes, but rather for propaganda and some payback for the brutal bombings of London.

"We had completed our run, and were headed back home over the channel when a flock of Me-109s appeared out of nowhere. It was like a gorgeous fireworks display with our fighters knocking them out of the sky when suddenly our plane was hit.

"A single Me-109 had escaped the destruction of his comrades and fired before he too bit the dust. When the shells impacted, it shook our aircraft, and we were ready to go swimming. Miraculously, there was no explosion or fire, and we were somehow able to limp back. Later, when the 20mm shells were examined, we learned the Source of our good fortune. The shells were found to be empty of any explosive charge, but one contained a rolled-up letter in English."

This is a letter to my only daughter, Rivka Schoenstein. The date is sometime in June or July of 1943. My name is Moshe Schoenstein, and I am an inmate in the Dachau Concentration Camp. I and several other men have been granted a temporary reprieve from the gas chambers to work in a nearby munitions factory. Our job is to load cartridges with explosives. I have loaded this letter into an empty shell in the hope with God's help that your aircraft will be saved and that this message will be retrieved and somehow make its way to my daughter.

Philip M. Fishman

To my darling daughter, Rivka, a few years after we sent you on your way to England, your mother and I were arrested and sent to this hell hole. Your mother is in heaven now, and I expect to join her shortly, but there is something that I hope you will be able to do if by some miracle that you receive this letter. All of the Nazis will receive their comeuppance in hell, but there is one man who deserves his hell on earth. You know who he is. He is the man that raped you on the night of Kristallnacht, and aside from being complicit in the mass execution of our fellow Jews, I saw him kill a friend of mine in cold blood. The man's name was Haim Goldberg. Stahl put his Luger to my friend's head and pulled the trigger because I had spit in Stahl's face. I don't care how you might arrange it, but I want him to suffer in agonizing pain before he dies. I realize that I am placing an enormous responsibility on you, but I trust that you feel the same.

I love you dearly.

      Papa

Did you recognize the name of the junior reporter?

She was Nate Levinson's niece and the wife of Alex Greenbaum. Nate and Rivka had fixed Alex up with Wendy on a blind date two years earlier when Nate's brother Jeff and his family came for a visit. Wendy had never known Rivka's maiden name, and when Alex saw the article, he had to call his mother first before filling Wendy in on the rest of the story.

After getting word from Alex, Rivka rushed to Steve's office to receive the fax from Alex. Rivka and Steve were both in tears as she read aloud the letter from her father. When she finished, she uttered the famous Hebrew prayer, "Shema Yisrael, Adonoi Elohenu, Adonoi Echod. It is done, Papa."

Acknowledgments

Thanks to all my beta readers, editors, and others who read all or part of my manuscript, correcting typos, smoothing out dialogue and encouraging me with their favorable comments. Debbie Allen, Angie Bryant, Richard Caldwell, Kathy Cameron, Tony Ciccone, Donald Dorfman. Pat and George Gissel, Willy Glen, Renee Haag, Marge Harris, Anna Holloway, Rosemary Jacobs, Paul V. Kelley, Laura Lyndhurst, Wesley Marsh, Jane McDonnold, Hilda Perkins, Lisa Evans Phillips, Gary Reiner, Judy Rofe, Kate Sampsell, Bertha Smith, Suzanne Sneed, Denise Wadsworth Trimm, Alicia Van Pelt, my daughter Missy Wilson and son-in-law Greg Wilson, Carole Wolf, Zoe Zefo.

Very special thanks to the following:

Nicole Jakub for her meticulous attention to detail in the final edit and smoothing out all the many wrinkles.

Dee Marley of White Rabbit Arts - Historical Book Company for the fabulous book cover design.

Debbie Burke at www.queenestherpublishing.com for editing, interior formatting, and the magnificent foreword.

Philip M. Fishman

Philip M. Fishman graduated from Indiana University in 1961 with a degree in chemistry. He served two years in the U.S. Army Chemical Corps as an executive officer in a technical intelligence detachment. Following his discharge, he worked in sales and marketing management in the chemical industry for forty years, followed by short stints as a consultant and teacher until his wife's stroke in 2008. Since then, he has doubled as a caregiver for her and a writer. This is his seventh published book, but he has written a number of short stories and is an active contributor on Facebook, primarily political commentary, as time permits.